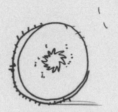  

    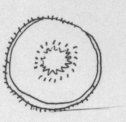

PRINCESSES
Save the World

SAVANNAH GUTHRIE and **ALLISON OPPENHEIM**
Illustrated by **EVA BYRNE**

Abrams Books for Young Readers · New York

For Vale and Charley, who always save the day
— S. G.

For Noah
— A. O.

The art in this book was created digitally.

Cataloging-in-Publication Data has been applied for and may be obtained
from the Library of Congress.

ISBN 978-1-4197-3171-6

Text and illustrations copyright © 2018 Savannah Guthrie and Allison Oppenheim
Book design by Pamela Notarantonio

Printed and bound in U.S.A.
10 9 8 7 6 5 4 3 2 1

Abrams Books for Young Readers are available at special discounts when purchased
in quantity for premiums and promotions as well as fundraising or educational use.
Special editions can also be created to specification. For details, contact
specialsales@abramsbooks.com or the address below.

Abrams® is a registered trademark of Harry N. Abrams, Inc.

ABRAMS The Art of Books
195 Broadway, New York, NY 10007
abramsbooks.com

WELCOME BACK, FRIENDS OF PRINCESS PENELOPE!
THERE'S MORE OF HER STORY TO TELL, YOU SEE.
TURN THE PAGE FOR THIS TALE OF OUR PINEAPPLE GIRL,
SO BRAVE AND QUICK-THINKING SHE SAVED THE FRUIT WORLD.

Princess Penelope Pineapple loved to bake.
She was known far and wide for her pineapple cake.
The secret ingredient in this signature treat:
Honey from her beehives, golden and sweet.

Penny loved to garden, to plant, and to sow.
In the Pineapple Kingdom, anything could grow.
But what made her kingdom so lush and alive
Were the bees of the royal Pineapple beehives.

She'd bring veggies to market and bouquets to her mother
Thanks to bees carrying pollen from one plant to another.

Penny's kingdom was colorful!
Orange, green, and blue–
Peonies, parsnips, and pumpkins, too!

One day, the princess, at work at the hive,
Received a rather shocking surprise.
Miss Fussy, with an envelope signed SOS:
A message from the Strawberry Kingdom in distress!

The royal duo took off in a jiffy.
In matching sailor suits, they felt quite spiffy.
As they cruised across the Fruitissippi River,
What Penny saw next gave her a shiver.

"Thank the stars, you're here," Princess Sabrina Strawberry sighed.
"Our fruit is all gone!" she said as she cried.
She pointed to fields of empty vines
Where berries once thrived in the warm sunshine.

"Something's wrong," she said. "I planted my seeds,
But the only things growing are tangled-up weeds!
None of our crops are healthy this year,
There's no fruit, no jam, no *smoothies*, I fear!"

"Without bees, we can't pollinate all the flowers.
We need some new hives and a good rain shower."
Penny's eyes lit up—she had bees in her care.
With millions at home, she'd have plenty to share!

The Pineapple Princess knew just what to do:
She'd call every other princess she knew.

"We'll be back!" she said to her friend in need,
And with Miss Fussy at the helm, they sailed home at top speed.

Back home and wearing her thinking glasses,
Penny began gathering the royal lasses.
This job would need teamwork and cooperation.
"A princess conference this Friday! *Calling all Fruit Nations!*"

Princess Beatrice Blueberry made the quickest time,
With regal Rita Raspberry not far behind.

Kira Kiwi rolled in on bright-green wheels,
With Maribel Mango hot on her heels.

Next to arrive was Princess Audrey Apple.
With her own fruit problems she, too, had grappled.
"Princesses!" she said. "You should've seen my sad orchard!
The trees were half-bare, and the fruit looked tortured."

"Bees were the answer," Princess Apple agreed.
"So let's all bring bees to the kingdom in need."
"Are you in?" Penny asked, with fingers crossed.
"We must work together, or all will be lost!"

One after the other, ladies reported for duty.
Princess Plum raised a cup to all things fruity!

The princesses, united, did a happy dance.
They loved to help others, and this was their chance!

Princess Blueberry gathered supplies
While Princess Apple supervised.
They created new hives for Penelope's bees
To travel across the river with ease.

"Just one question," a small voice was heard to say.
"How will we get the bees to come our way?"
Little Princess Grape had a point to be made.
You can't *tell* bees what to do—you have to persuade!

Just then Penny took charge of the matter.
Her voice rang out above all the chatter.
"I've long cared for bees, and I know them well.
If there's one thing they'll follow, it's an alluring smell!"

Penny encouraged the princesses to look
For anything fragrant that might work as a hook.
Out of their bags they pulled all things smelly:
Perfume! Peppermints! Peanut butter and jelly!

Penny and Miss Fussy went straight to their lab,
Created a scent, and then, with a dab,
They tested what would happen when it hit the air.
It worked! One squirt, and bees swarmed everywhere!

With Eau de Bee-utiful, Penelope led the way,
And the bees buzzed on over to follow her spray.
Each princess then ran to grab an oar
To row the new hives to Strawberry Shores.

Princess Strawberry let out a joyful cry
As the boat reached the dock and bees filled the sky.
"You did it!" she squealed to the girls with glee.
"Thank goodness for Penelope, our real Queen Bee!"

One year later, with the strawberries now hearty,
Sabrina hosted a princess tea party.

Each one arrived to present a surprise—
Her kingdom's very own homemade fruit pies!

Now every year on that day they remember their feat,
And that fruit is delicious, and friendship so sweet!

BEES SAVE THE WORLD!

Did you know that honeybees are some of the sweetest members of our ecosystem? They work hard to pollinate all kinds of plants—from apples to strawberries to sunflowers, and everything in between! Without bees, some of your favorite fruits, vegetables, and flowers wouldn't be able to grow.

Pollination is an important process that helps plants grow big and strong. Without pollination, no new plants—like Princess Sabrina's strawberries—would blossom. Some plants can be pollinated by the wind, but others need to be pollinated by insects. And the very best pollinators are honeybees. Honeybees are drawn to plants with bright colors and strong smells. They drink up some of the nectar that the plant has to offer. While they're snacking on the nectar, some of the plant's pollen gets stuck to their legs and feet. Then, when they land on the next plant or flower for another snack, that pollen gets a new home. Now the new plant is pollinated, or fertilized, so it can grow to its fullest potential—with tons of fruit or flowers to offer.

Unfortunately, Princess Sabrina Strawberry's bee crisis has become all too common. Due to many factors—such as environmental changes and the use of pesticides that are harmful to bees—the number of honeybees that are around to pollinate crops is rapidly dwindling. To learn more and to find out how you can help, ask your teacher or a local librarian to direct you to some books or online resources about honeybees.

    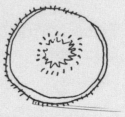

   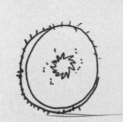  

  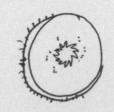 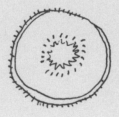